Frank Rodgers

The Witch's Dog
and the
Crystal Ball

PUFFIN BOOKS

PUFFIN BOOKS

Published by the Penguin Group
Penguin Books Ltd, 27 Wrights Lane, London W8 5TZ, England
Penguin Putnam Inc., 375 Hudson Street, New York, New York 10014, USA
Penguin Books Australia Ltd, Ringwood, Victoria, Australia
Penguin Books Canada Ltd, 10 Alcorn Avenue, Toronto, Ontario, Canada M4V 3B2
Penguin Books India (P) Ltd, 11 Community Centre, Panchsheel Park,
New Delhi – 110 017, India
Penguin Books (NZ) Ltd, Cnr Rosedale and Airborne Roads, Albany,
Auckland, New Zealand
Penguin Books (South Africa) (Pty) Ltd, 5 Watkins Street, Denver Ext 4,
Johannesburg 2094, South Africa

On the World Wide Web at: www.penguin.com

Penguin Books Ltd, Registered Offices: Harmondsworth, Middlesex, England

First published 2000
5 7 9 10 8 6 4

Printed in Hong Kong by Midas Printing Ltd

British Library Cataloguing in Publication Data
A CIP catalogue record for this book is available from the British Library

ISBN 0–141–30656–4

Wilf, the Witch's Dog, was
playing football in the garden
with his friends – Bertie, Harry and
Streaky.

1

"That's not fair," he panted, as Streaky took the ball off him for the tenth time.

"Your legs are a lot longer than mine."

His friends laughed.

"Let's have a rest then," said Bertie.

"Good idea," said
Wilf. "I'm hot.
Who'd like some
lemonade?"

"Me!" cried Bertie, Harry and
Streaky together.

"I'll go and get some," said Wilf,
and went into the kitchen.

3

Weenie the Witch was sitting at the
kitchen table. She looked very
unhappy.

Wilf forgot about the lemonade.
"What's wrong, Weenie?" he asked.
"Aren't you feeling well?"

4

Weenie sighed. "I'm fine, Wilf," she said. "It's just that today is the Witches' Fun Day."

"Is it?" cried Wilf. "Brilliant!"

Weenie sighed again.

"Not so brilliant, Wilf," she said.
"You see, all the witches bring a
special magic thing they have
created ... but I can't think
what to make this year.

"The witch who
makes the best
thing is crowned
'Queen of the
Fun Day'."

"Have you ever been crowned
'Queen of the Fun Day', Weenie?"
asked Wilf.

"No," said
Weenie. "All
the magic
things I made
were faulty.

"One year I made a tiny broomstick
– but it flew up a wizard's nose.

"Another time I made a flying
carpet – but all it did was hop about
like a flat frog. Everybody
laughed."

"What a shame,"
said Wilf.

8

Just then they heard Bertie shout:
"Goal!" and the next moment ...

a football
shot through the
open window and
landed

in Weenie's
cauldron.

"Oops, sorry," said Bertie, looking in at the window. "I don't know my own strength."

Wilf fished the dripping ball out of the cauldron.

Suddenly his eyes lit up. "Weenie!" he cried. "I've just had a great idea for the Fun Day!

Why don't you turn this into a crystal ball? You know, the kind that shows the future."

Weenie gasped in delight.
"Yes!" she
cried. "That *is*
a great idea.
Wilf, you're a
genius!"

Putting the ball
into an empty
pot, she opened
her book of
magic.

"Here goes," Weenie said. She began to pour magic potions on to the ball.

Steam rose from the pot, misting up Weenie's glasses.

While Weenie was busy making the
spell, Harry said, "I've heard about
the Witches' Fun Day, Wilf. They
have music and magic –"

"And sports where you aren't allowed to use magic," said Bertie.

"I wouldn't need magic," said Streaky. "I'm as fast as the wind."

"I'm as slow as tomato sauce," said Wilf. At that moment ...

15

BANG!

There was a bright blue flash from Weenie's pot and the kitchen filled with smoke.

"Are you all right, Weenie?" gasped Wilf.
Weenie nodded ...

then out of the pot she lifted a
shining, glittering crystal ball.

"You've done
it, Weenie!"
cried Wilf.
"Brilliant!"

17

Weenie smiled proudly and peered
at the ball.
"It works!" she said.

"I can see me making the spell ...
Now I can see you coming into the
kitchen, Wilf."

18

Her face fell.
"Oh no!" she cried. "It's working
backwards!

The crystal ball is showing things
that have already happened. It
doesn't show the future at all!"

Weenie sat down at the table
looking very glum.
"The other
witches are
going to laugh
at me again,"
she said.

"Let's check the spell," said Wilf.
"Perhaps you missed something
out."

Weenie shook her head and wiped her steamed-up glasses.

"No, Wilf," she sighed. "It's just that my magic has gone wrong again. We'll go to the Fun Day without the crystal ball."

The Fun Day was very jolly. There were balloons and bunting and music and coloured lights.

Near the entrance was a gallery of pictures of famous witches' pets.

Wilf looked at them and sighed.
"There are pictures of rats, cats,
bats, toads and spiders," he said
sadly, "but still no dogs."

"That's because a dog is a useless
thing to have as a witch's pet," said
a voice behind them.

Wilf turned round and saw Sly Cat
and Tricky Toad. They were
witches' pets too – and they hated
the idea of Wilf becoming better
than them at magic.

"I don't know why you came to the
Fun Day," sneered Sly. "A witch's
dog is no use at anything."

"No use at anything," echoed
Tricky, with a snigger. "Not even
sports."

And off they went, snorting with
laughter.

"Pests!" muttered Bertie, and Wilf
frowned.
"I'll show
them!" he said.
"I'm going to
enter the
sports and win
something!"

"Go for it,
Wilf!" said his
friends.
So Wilf put
his name
down for the
sprint race,
the long jump
and the ball-
throwing
event.

26

Streaky showed him how to run fast.

"Like this!" he said, and zoomed off.

Wilf practised ... and in the race he tried hard ...

but he came last.

"I used to jump on the ice all the time back home," said Harry. "I'll show you how to do it."

Wilf practised ... and in the long jump he tried even harder ...

but he came last in that too.

Then Bertie showed him how to throw the ball.

Wilf practised ...

"I think you might win this time," said Weenie.

Sly and Tricky heard this.
"We'd better stop him," muttered
Tricky, but Sly grinned.

"No," he said.
"We'll make *sure*
he wins ... by
magic! That way
he'll be
disqualified!"

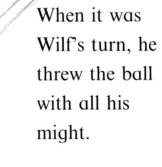

When it was
Wilf's turn, he
threw the ball
with all his
might.

It looked like the
winning throw –

but as it flew
through the air,
Sly and Tricky
secretly
put a spell on it
and ...

ZOOM

the ball
picked up speed and
landed in the next field.
The judge frowned.

"There was magic
in that ball," she
said. "And magic
isn't allowed in the
sports. You are
disqualified, Wilf."

"But –" said Wilf.

"No buts!" said the judge. "You broke the rules.

"You are out of the sports because you cheated."

Wilf trudged away miserably.

"I think Sly and Tricky are to blame," said Weenie. "But how can we prove it?"

Just then there was an
announcement.
"It's time for the
display! Would
all witches please
bring their magic
creations to the
stage."

Weenie sniffed. "I wish my crystal ball had worked properly," she said.

Wilf snapped his fingers.

"Aha!" he exclaimed. "That gives me an idea!"

35

Wilf turned to Streaky. "Could you rush back to Weenie's house and fetch the crystal ball and the magic book, please, Streaky?"

"Just watch me," replied Streaky and . . .

ZOOM

. . . he shot away at top speed.

"But, Wilf," protested Weenie, "the witches will laugh at my backward crystal ball – you know they will!"

"We'll see," said Wilf mysteriously. "We'll see."

For the display, the other witches
had brought along some wonderful
things –
a bottle of rainbow
lemonade in
seven different
flavours ...

an everlasting ice
cream ...

a magic paintbrush ...

38

a flying umbrella for people with their hands full …

and a clock that really told the time.

Weenie sighed. "They're all so good, Wilf," she said. "I hope Streaky doesn't get back in time with my silly ball."

WHOOSH

Streaky skidded to
a halt beside them
with the book and
the crystal ball.

"Here you are," he said, hardly out
of breath. "No problem!"
"Thanks, Streaky," said Wilf. He
looked at the spells in the book and
grinned.

"You must enter the crystal ball in the display, Weenie," he said.
Weenie sighed again.
"All right, Wilf," she said. "I just hope you know what you're doing."

The judge peered into the crystal
ball, then shook her head.
"This works backwards, Weenie,"
she said.

The other witches began to
laugh ...

but the judge stared into the ball
again.

"Wait a moment," she said. "What's
this? I can see Wilf throwing the
ball . . .

and I can see
Sly and
Tricky putting
a spell on it!"

The audience gasped.

"You two are the cheats ... not
Wilf!" the judge said angrily,
pointing at Sly and Tricky.

"You should
be ashamed of
yourselves!"

44

Sly and Tricky slunk off in disgrace. "Who would have thought that Wilf would have a crystal ball that worked backwards?" Sly muttered in disgust.

"You just never know what that dog is going to do next," moaned Tricky.

"I'm sorry for my mistake," said the judge, turning to Wilf.

"That's all right," replied Wilf, opening Weenie's book of magic and pointing to a spell.

"Weenie got this spell wrong
because her glasses steamed up," he
explained.
"Can I fix it?"
"Please do," said
the judge.

So Wilf read the spell out very
carefully and ...

The judge looked into the crystal
ball and beamed.

"It works!" she
cried.

"I can see what's going to
happen next!"

48

Then her eyes grew wide. "Oh no!" she said. "Bad news! There's going to be a sudden storm that will completely wash away the Fun Day!"

Everyone looked up ...

and sure enough there was a huge
black cloud overhead.

Suddenly there was a loud

CRAAACK!

And bolts of lightning came
shooting down from the cloud.

Everyone gasped and stood frozen
to the spot. They couldn't think
what to do ... but Weenie could.
Quickly she sent out a spell.

The cloud exploded into a million
stars . . .

and the lightning bolts were
transformed into the best fireworks
display anyone had ever seen.

The witches and their pets cheered
wildly.

"Hooray for Weenie!" they yelled.

The judge beamed.
"Your magic has saved the Fun
Day from disaster, Weenie," she
said. "Thank you.

"And, of course, we must thank Wilf
too!

"Weenie, I hereby crown you . . .
Queen of the Fun Day."

Everyone cheered again and Weenie
blushed with pride.

"You're a
genius, Wilf,"
she whispered.

Wilf was given a special award. His picture was added to the gallery of famous witches' pets.

The judge smiled.
"There may be lots of rats, bats,
cats, toads and spiders," she said,

"but there's only one Wilf . . .

the world's first and *best* witch's dog!"